A Vacation for Pooch

Maryann Cocca-Leffler

Christy Ottaviano Books

Henry Holt and Company ● New York

Henry Holt and Company, LLC
Publishers since 1866
175 Fifth Avenue
New York, New York 10010
mackids.com

Library of Congress Cataloging-in-Publication Data
Cocca-Leffler, Maryann, 1958-
A vacation for Pooch / Maryann Cocca-Leffler. — 1st ed.
        p.   cm.
"Christy Ottaviano Books."
Summary: Violet is unhappy that her dog cannot join her on vacation at the beach, but Pooch is having fun on
Grandpa's farm, despite the fact that Violet accidentally took the bag with Pooch's favorite toys and treats.
ISBN 978-0-8050-9106-9 (hardcover)
[1. Vacations—Fiction. 2. Dogs—Fiction.] I. Title.
PZ7.C638Vac 2013   [E]—dc23   2012011271

First Edition—2013 / Designed by Véronique Lefèvre Sweet

The artist used gouache with fabric collage on watercolor paper
to create the illustrations for this book.

Printed in China by Toppan Leefung Printing Ltd., Dongguan City, Guangdong Province

1   3   5   7   9   10   8   6   4   2

To my daughter, Kristin,
and her best friends, Stephanie and Mallory—
Even when distance separates you, you'll always be close.
Love, MCL

Violet packed two bags. In one bag she packed her doll, Molly, crayons, drawing paper, and her favorite books.

And in the other, she packed a leash, dog food, a red ball, and Pooch's stuffed cat.

Pooch ran back and forth to the door, wagging his tail. "Mommy, why can't we take Pooch on vacation with us?" asked Violet.

Pooch looked up.
Violet looked down.

"We can't take a dog
to Florida," Mom said.
"Pooch will have his
own vacation on
Grandpa's farm."

"It won't be a good
vacation for Pooch,"
said Violet. "He'll miss
me the whole time!"

"I can't bring you.
No dogs allowed." Violet
sniffed.

When Grandpa arrived,
Violet gave him Pooch's bag.
   "Pooch won't sleep without
his stuffed toy, Fluffy Cat."
   "Okay," said Grandpa.

"And Pooch likes to play catch with his favorite red ball right after lunch."

"Got it."

"And make sure you use his leash when you take him for a walk or he'll run into the woods."

"Violet, don't worry about a thing," said Grandpa. "Just have fun!"

Through the truck window, Violet said good-bye to Pooch.

Soon Pooch was on his way to the farm.

And Violet was on her way to the beach.

That afternoon, Violet played in the pool.

Later at the beach, Violet met a new friend.

At dinner, Violet ate lots of exciting foods.

Then Violet went for a
long walk on the beach.

That night, Violet snuggled into her big, fancy bed.

She got her bag and reached for her doll, Molly,
and pulled out . . .

FLUFFY CAT!

"Mom! Dad!

I have Pooch's bag.

I have Pooch's ball . . .

and food . . .

and leash . . .

and sleepy toy!

This is horrible!

While I was playing . . .

Pooch was

BORED!

While I was with my new friend . . .

Pooch was

LONELY!

While I was eating . . .

Pooch was

FEED ME

STARVING!

While I was walking on the beach . . .

Pooch was

LOST IN THE WOODS!

While I was having FUN, Pooch was MISERABLE!

I WANT TO GO HOME!"

"Let's call Grandpa," said Mom.

"Hello, Grandpa. Did you find Pooch?"

"Hello?"

"Find him? He's right here, sleeping at my feet."

"SLEEPING?

How can he be sleeping?
I have his sleepy toy, Fluffy Cat."

"Pooch is tired. He was playing in the field all afternoon."

"PLAYING?

What did he play with? I have his favorite red ball."

"Pooch didn't need his ball. He found a friend."

"FRIEND?

How can he have a friend? I'm his best friend."

"You bet, but now he has another friend. And they had dinner together."

"DINNER?

What dinner? I have his dog food."

"Oh, this was a special dinner— homemade beef stew. Pooch is fine. He's having fun."

"FUN?

Doesn't he miss me?"

"Of course he misses you, but he has
your doll, Molly, to keep him company."

"And that you do!
Good night, Violet."

"Good night, Grandpa."